BL 3.3 LY
pts 0.5

Dani Binns
Practical Paramedic

CW00951934

Written by Lisa Rajan

Illustrated by Alessia Trunfio

Collins

Chapter 1

Dani Binns stepped into the spare bedroom, looking for the old toy box.

"See you later, Tara," she called to her big sister. "It's playtime!"

"OK …" smiled Tara, "… but be back before bedtime."

Every time Dani took a toy out of the box, she was sent off on an adventure to try out a different job.

Back before bedtime … thought Dani, as she spied a cuddly teddy bear lying on top of the other toys. She lifted it out.

Her hand began to tingle. The tingling spread up her arm and around her whole body. Then she began spinning and tumbling through space and time …

Chapter 2

When the world stopped spinning, Dani could hear the piercing noise of a siren wailing overhead.

She was sitting in an ambulance, speeding through traffic. Cars moved aside to let the ambulance pass.

"Hi, Dani!" said the girl to her left.
"I'm Asha and this is Tai. There has been
a bike accident. A girl has been injured."

"You won't need a teddy," said Tai, handing her
a case full of medical equipment. "It usually takes
more than a cuddle for paramedics like us to make
things better!"

"Over here!" shouted a boy, frantically waving his arms.

Asha pulled over by the park entrance. Dani and Tai jumped out and ran over to him.

The boy led them along the park path to where a girl was lying. She wasn't moving. Her bike lay awkwardly on the ground nearby. Her helmet had been thrown clear and lay upturned on the path ahead.

Tai dropped to his knees to examine her.

"Hello, we're paramedics, here to help," he said. "Can you hear me?"

The girl stirred but didn't answer.

"What happened?" Dani asked the boy.

"She was riding into the park, quite fast. She swerved to avoid me and flew over the handlebars. I think she landed on her head. I told her not to move. Then I called for an ambulance," he replied.

"You did the right thing, telling her not to move," said Tai. "If she landed on her head, she might have injured her neck or back. That's very serious."

Asha checked the girl's pulse and breathing. Then she put an inflating cuff around the girl's arm to check her blood pressure. Tai shone a mini torch in her eyes to check her reactions.

The girl muttered something. It sounded like "Benny".

"What's your name?" Tai asked her, gently.

"It's … it's … *err* … Jenny," she answered, shakily.

"Where does it hurt, Jenny?" Tai continued.

"My head. Here –" Jenny winced and started to raise her hand to show him.

"Don't move!" said Asha, quickly. "You might make the injury worse. Can you just tell us, without showing us?"

"*Err ... at the ... near my –*" started Jenny. She looked confused and helpless.

How can I help her? wondered Dani, squeezing the teddy anxiously.

Of course – the teddy!

She knelt down in front of Jenny.

"I'm Dani and this is Teddy," she said. "Perhaps we can help you to show us. Did you hurt yourself here?" Dani pointed to the back of the teddy's head.

"No," whimpered Jenny.

"Here?" asked Dani, pointing to its ear.

"No."

Dani pointed to the teddy's forehead, above its right eye.

"Here?"

Chapter 3

"Y-yes, there," said Jenny.

Asha gently pushed Jenny's hair back and found a bump on her forehead. Jenny winced and started crying.

"Is … is Benny OK?" she sobbed fearfully. "Anything broken? Scratches?"

Dani looked up at the boy to check.

"I'm fine," he shrugged, "but I'm not Benny. My name is Karim."

"Was there someone with her when she crashed?" puzzled Tai. "Another boy, perhaps?"

Karim shook his head. "No, just me."

Dani frowned. *Who was Benny then?*

"She could be confused from the head injury," stated Asha. "We should get her to the hospital."

13

Tai went to fetch the gurney from the ambulance.
Asha checked the rest of Jenny's head for bruises.

"Were you wearing a helmet?" she asked gently.

"Yes," replied Jenny, sobbing again.

Asha picked it up, looking for damage.
There wasn't any.

"Does it hurt anywhere else?" asked Dani, showing
Jenny the teddy again. "Here? Or here? Or here?"

Jenny said, "Yes," when Dani pointed to the teddy's arm and leg. Asha checked Jenny's knee and wrist. Both looked swollen and grazed.

Tai came back with a head immobiliser. He fitted it around Jenny's head and shoulders, so that they wouldn't move when she was lifted on to the gurney.

"Benny!" Jenny called out, as they wheeled her towards the ambulance. "We can't leave Benny behind!"

"Lenny will be angry with me!" Jenny was very upset now. She kept trying to raise her head to look at Karim.

Now there's an imaginary Lenny, as well as an imaginary Benny! thought Dani.

Dani scanned the park to look for other boys nearby, in case Jenny had been with someone else when she crashed. There was no one around.

Asha looked worried.

"I think her head injury may be even more serious than we first thought. Let's get her to the hospital quickly."

Dani gave Jenny the teddy to hold. She hoped it would help calm Jenny down a bit.

Something doesn't quite make sense, she thought.

Dani went over everything in her mind as she helped Karim pick up Jenny's bike.

Aside from Lenny and Benny, Jenny doesn't seem confused, Dani considered. *She could answer questions about her injuries, after all …*

"What a cool bike!" commented Karim. "I have one just like it. Benning is one of the best bike makers."

"It does look too big for her, though," he continued. "Maybe that's why she crashed."

Dani hung the helmet on the handlebars. She noticed that the strap clip was still done up.

So why did the helmet come off her head when she fell off?

Chapter 4

Dani thought about what Karim had just said ... about the bike being too big for Jenny.

Maybe the helmet was too big as well? That would explain why it had fallen off her head when she fell.

That was why she had a bump on her forehead but there was no damage to the helmet!

Dani linked it together. *If both the bike and the helmet were too big for Jenny, maybe they didn't belong to her? Maybe she had borrowed them from someone else?*

Dani looked into the helmet. There was a name written inside it.

"Lenny!" Dani read.

Dani looked at the bike again. The brand name was written on the crossbar … Benning …

It came to her in a flash!

"Asha!" Dani called over to the ambulance. "Ask Jenny if Benny is the bike. And does it belong to someone else?"

Asha relayed the question. Dani ran over to hear the answer.

"Yes … Benny is my older brother's bike," replied Jenny, biting her lip.

"Is your brother called Lenny?" asked Dani, slotting in another piece of the puzzle.

"Yes, but I borrowed his bike without asking," Jenny said guiltily. "He'll be annoyed if it's scratched or damaged."

"The bike's fine," Dani reassured her. "No bumps or scratches. I'll make sure Lenny gets it back, although I'm sure he'll be more concerned about you than the bike."

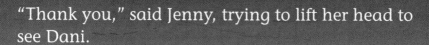

"Thank you," said Jenny, trying to lift her head to see Dani.

"You must keep still, Jenny," said Tai. "You might have other injuries that we can't see. You don't want to make anything worse. The hospital will check you over thoroughly."

"At least the confusion is cleared up!" said Asha, kindly.

Jenny handed the teddy to Asha. "Will you give this back to Dani for me, please?"

"I was wrong …" Tai said to Dani, "… you did need your teddy, after all. And we needed both of you. Your practical idea to help Jenny tell us where she was hurt without moving was really important. You helped keep her safe."

"Here you go," said Asha, handing Dani the teddy. "You'll both sleep well tonight!"

As Dani took the teddy from her, she felt a tingle in her hand ... then her arm. Then her whole body started spinning and tumbling, away from the ambulance ...

KA-BOOM!

Chapter 5

When the spinning stopped, Dani found herself back in the spare bedroom. Her sister Tara was waiting for her. She squeezed the teddy tight to thank him for his help.

"What an exciting adventure!" Dani told Tara, proudly. "Teddy and I helped a girl who fell off her bike."

Dani put the teddy back in the toy box. "We worked out what was wrong without moving a muscle! The girl's muscles, that is – she had to keep still, you see. Maybe I'll be a paramedic when I grow up."

"You're full of practical ideas, Dani," smiled Tara, closing the lid. "And it sounds like the toy box gave you the perfect little emergency helper."

How did Dani work out where Jenny was hurt?

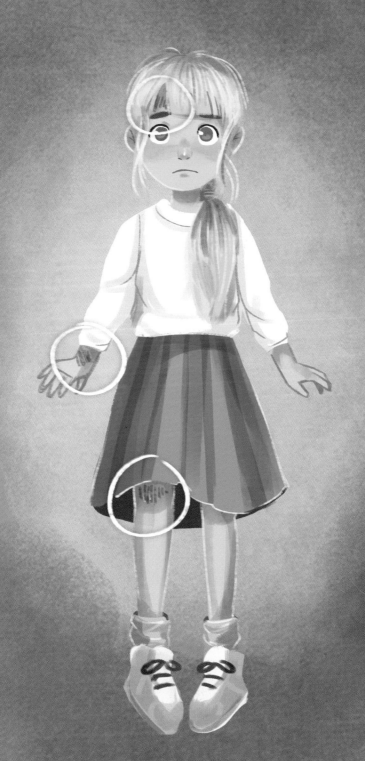

Ideas for reading

Written by Clare Dowdall, PhD
Lecturer and Primary Literacy Consultant

Reading objectives:

- discuss the sequence of events in books and how items of information are related
- make inferences on the basis of what is being said and done
- answer and ask questions

Spoken language objectives:

- maintain attention and participate actively in collaborative conversations, staying on topic and initiating and responding to comments
- participate in discussions, presentations, performances and debates

Curriculum links: PSHE: Health and wellbeing; Relationships

Interest words: paramedic, piercing, medical, pulse, cuff, blood pressure, gurney, head immobiliser

Resources: paper and pencils for drawing and writing

Build a context for reading

- Look at the front cover and read the title *Practical Paramedic*. Ask children to suggest what being *practical* means. Use an example, e.g. the teacher was very practical.
- Read the blurb to the group. Ask children to describe what they think paramedics do and to suggest what skills and qualities they might need to be good at their job.
- Introduce the interest words and help children to read and understand any that are unfamiliar.
- If appropriate, ask children about how they keep safe when out on their bikes, and about any experiences with paramedics (sensitivity needed).

Understand and apply reading strategies

- Ask for a volunteer to read pp2–5 to the group. Ask another volunteer to explain what has happened and suggest whether Tai's comment about a paramedic needing a teddy is right or not.